Pulling Weeds

Pulling Weeds

CULTIVATING FOR CHRISTIAN GROWTH

Les Morgan

CHRISTIAN PUBLICATIONS

CAMP HILL, PENNSYLVANIA

Christian Publications
3825 Hartzdale Drive, Camp Hill, PA 17011

The mark of  vibrant faith

ISBN: 0-87509-414-7
LOC Catalog Card Number: 88-93031
© 1989 by Christian Publications
All rights reserved
Printed in the United States of America

· 93 92   5 4 3 2

To Kay
Who encouraged me to keep
on working,
Who believed in me when
I didn't even believe in myself,
Who loved me through
the times when I had to "pull
weeds" from my own life.

CONTENTS

———

Preface

You are about to hear from someone very grateful to God: me! In the darkest hours of my trying to put this material together, a verse from Second Corinthians was an assuring light: "Now he who supplies seed to the sower and bread for food will also supply and increase your store of seed and will enlarge the harvest of your righteousness" (9:10).

Also, I cannot adequately say thanks to Fred Hartley for his work on the manuscript. His willingness to wade through the stuff over and over again speaks of his dedication to the project and of our friendship.

My challenge to you as this book heads to press is to excell in Jesus Christ. Be all you can for His soon-coming kingdom. When all is said and done and the dust settles, the only thing left standing will be God's truth. Since that is so, start now to pull those weeds that keep you from following Jesus fully.

Les Morgan
Toccoa Falls College
Toccoa, Georgia

Foreword

When I first met Les Morgan, he was a long-haired weight lifter who drove a jacked-up white jeep and strutted around with a girl hanging on each arm. If you would have told me then that I would some day write the foreword to his first book, I would have called the game warden to come and put you out of your misery.

Les Morgan knows his subject. He knows what it is to pull weeds; he has pulled a few out of his own life. One of my great joys has been to watch God remove those weeds and make Les like a "well-watered garden."

Les also knows his audience. It is obvious that he has spent years of ministry down in the trenches with young people.

The book is fast-moving, racing from one good story to another without getting stuck in the mud. The author doesn't preach. He paints pictures—pictures in which we can all see ourselves. This book is not just a lot of theory. It is real life.

Fred Hartley
Homestead, Florida

Dare to Sweat

W illiam was a typical kid. He went to school, cut the grass and fed the dog. He was not an exceptional student, so he had to work hard for good grades. He hated going to the dentist and occasionally got into mischief. He liked girls and sports, especially baseball. He even thought of working toward the majors.

He went to church but wasn't excited about it. In fact, he thought of church as something only for women and "sissies." To him, reading the Bible and prayer were all "hogwash."

One day, though, he learned that Jesus Christ could make a difference in his life. He had heard about Christ before, but the message never had much of an impact on him. This time, however, William responded and made Jesus his Lord. His theory that Christianity was only for women and "sissies" went down the drain. Now, he was a Christian, and he found it to be an exciting experience— more exciting even than when he shook hands with his idol, Babe Ruth.

Soon William began reading the Bible every day, and before long he had learned a few verses he could quote from memory. He started a Christian club in his high school and didn't even mind the heckling from his old friends. He was on the move for God.

He went to Bible college near Tampa, Florida, and started preaching in prisons and at youth rallies as God gave him opportunities. He refused to allow anything in his life that did not center on Jesus. The result? He has made the greatest impact for Christ since the Apostle Paul.

Who is this William? Billy Graham!

God hasn't called us all to be "supermen" and "wonder women" of the Christian faith, but He has called us to be faithful disciples. Doing this, though, isn't always an easy task to accomplish. "How do I become an effective disciple?" you might be asking. Part of the process is up to the Holy Spirit as He works to shape us into the image of Christ. The other part of the process is up to us. Remember the line from above: "He refused to allow anything in his life that did not center on Jesus." That's what this book is about—not allowing anything in our lives that pulls us away from Jesus.

In Mark 4, Jesus talks about this very thing.

Listen! A farmer decided to sow some grain. As he scattered it across his field, some of it fell on a path, and some birds came and picked it off the hard ground and ate it. Some fell on thin soil with underlying rock. It grew up quickly enough, but soon wilted beneath the hot sun and died because the roots had no nourishment in the soil. Other seeds *fell among the thorns that shot up and crowded the young plants so they produced no grain* [italics mine]. But some of the seed fell into good soil and yielded thirty times as much as he planted—some of it even sixty or a hundred times as much. . . . The farmer I talked about is anyone who brings God's message to others, trying to plant good seed within their lives. The hard pathway, where some of the seeds fell, represents the hearts of those who hear God's message; Satan comes at once to try to make them forget. The rocky soil represents the hearts of those who hear the message with joy, but, like young plants in such soil, their roots don't go very deep, and though at first they get along fine, as soon as persecution begins, they wilt. The thorny ground represents the hearts of people who listen to the Good News and receive it, but all too quickly the attractions of this world and the delights of wealth, and the search for success and the lure of nice things come in and crowd out God's message from their hearts, so that no crop is produced. But the good soil represents the hearts of those who truly accept God's message and produce a plentiful harvest for God—thirty, sixty, or even a hundred times as much as was planted in their hearts. (verses 3–8, 14–20, TLB)

When we receive Jesus as our Savior, it's as if good things are planted in our lives. So that these good things grow and produce fruit, they have to be cared for—just as crops that the farmer plants or flowers that a gardener grows have to be cared for. Part of that process is weeding. Weeds can choke and kill young plants, and they can rob mature plants of nourishment and water. The same thing can happen in our lives. Weeds or sins will choke out the good "seeds"—those things that keep our hearts and minds on Jesus Christ.

So we have to "pull weeds." Here's a simple formula to remember:

- Anything that gets in God's way is a weed and must go. It must be pulled up by its roots and tossed into the dumpster.
- Anything that helps us grow God's way gets cultivated, fertilized and cared for.

Origin of weeds

The dictionary defines *weed* as "a wild plant growing in a cultivated field and injurious to cultivated plants; unsightly, useless plants; anything useless or troublesome." Where did these pesky weeds come from anyway? The Bible answers our question in the horrible pronouncement Adam and Eve received as they were dismissed from the Garden of Eden. They had done the thing God said not to do. Now, they had to face His judgment.

To Adam God said,

Cursed is the ground because of you;
    through painful toil you will eat of it all the days
    of your life.
It will produce thorns and thistles for you. (Genesis
    3:17–18)

In other words, when sin entered the world, weeds came too. And, as we have said, weeds can be compared to the sins in our lives.

Jesus in His garden

The darkest hour Jesus faced was in the Garden of Gethsemene. Men had cultivated sin in their lives, and He came

6

to set them free. In the final moments before His betrayal, He prayed for God's will to be accomplished. He was gripped by man's bondage to sin and the inescapable penalty for disobeying God: death. As He faced the awfulness of sin, He sweat great drops of blood, and in His dying Jesus willingly exchanged His sinlessness for our sin. The thorns He wore on His forehead were symbolic of how He took the weeds of sin upon Himself when He died.

We are all familiar with pulling weeds. They grow in gardens, sidewalks, driveways and yards. What a drag!

I grew up in Florida where weeds grow 12 months a year. I soon found out that the best way for me to earn money was to do yard work around the neighborhood. One of my regular jobs was pulling weeds from neighbors' yards. Here are a few things I learned about weeds:

1. You don't have to plant weeds; they grow by themselves. They also can grow almost anywhere. I have seen them growing in a crack on a major highway.
2. When weeds grow, the lawn or garden suffers. Good plants and weeds don't mix. Why? Because the nutrients, proteins and water intended for the good plants are feeding the undesired weeds.
3. People *hate* weeds. They are willing to use weed-eaters, herbicides and even hire neighborhood boys to do the hot, sweaty work of weeding. They know that if the weeds don't go, the good plants won't grow.

Uprooting root systems

If we are not careful, instead of pulling "weeds" from our lives, we can actually cultivate them. Remember the dictionary definition of weeds—"anything useless and troublesome." Sin in our lives needs to be uprooted. Just as weeds take up the valuable nutrients that good plants need for growth, so too does sin keep us from the things we need to grow in God.

Most of us never intend for "weeds" to take root in our lives. But they do. Lawns are that way. No one intends for weeds to grow among the beautiful grass, but they always seem to pop up. Getting rid of them is hard work, but it must be done if the lawn is to look good. The same is true for the sin in our lives. It takes hard work to uproot sinful habits and thoughts, but if we want to grow in God, we have to root them out.

I remember my experiences at a youth camp in central Florida. A number of the teens attending the camp had "weeds" in their lives that needed pulling.

Because of a bad home life, Sally was withdrawn and rebellious toward her mom. After meeting God in a personal way, she called her mom at 11:30 one night and wept as she asked for forgiveness.

John had some friends who were a bad influence on him. God allowed him to see that those friendships were wrong. Now, he is determined to be different.

Mike had trouble sharing his faith with his buddies. After being confronted with Christ's command to tell the world the Good News, he discovered that, by not telling them about Jesus, he had not really been a friend at all.

Marie's dating life was a mess. Things had got out of line physically with her boyfriend. She asked God to show her what He wants in a relationship. Until then she is determined to back off from dating.

Gil had a hard time making time to read the Bible. To him, it had become stale. The reason: the trash on many television programs had become more important than the truth of God's Word. Gil decided to be selective in his television viewing and devote more time to God.

These and others like them are finding real joy as they pull the "weeds" that are holding them back spiritually. What a thrill!

Are you ready to do that in your life? I'm not talking about pulling the tops off weeds and leaving the roots. If that is your intent, forget it—you have lost already. But if you are ready to get serious about God and do some major "uprooting," then let's get started. It will take work, but it will be worth the effort as you see the difference in your life for Jesus.

Sizing up the task

You have to decide what happens in *your* life. No one else is able to make that decision. The Holy Spirit will show you what "weeds" need to be pulled. As you listen to and obey Him, you will grow to be all that God wants you to be. Weed-pulling is demanding, but with the goal of being all you can be for God, you can make it.

Archie Griffin, former Ohio State University halfback and only recipient of the Heisman Trophy award two years in a row, knows what hard work, determination and demands are all about. Coming from a poor black family

in Ohio, he realized that opportunity for him was some-
what limited. As a boy, he was overweight and clumsy.
His brothers nicknamed him "Butterball." One day, however, he decided he was going to change.

He started exercising, wearing dry cleaning bags and
his dad's old sweaters to make him sweat. He couldn't
afford barbells, so he filled two cases of Coke bottles with
sand and tied them to a pole. It was a demanding routine
lifting them into the air and back down again. He did sit-
ups and push-ups in an old, broken-down station wagon
that sat next to his house. In the winter when it was too
cold to be outside, he would turn on the hot water and
take a steam bath. He increased his agility by doing wind
sprints. Soon, he began to see positive changes.

He made his high school football team, and then was
able to make the Ohio State University football squad,
though he was on the fifth team. A Christian, Archie
asked the Lord from the beginning to help him keep his
priorities straight. He put crosses on each shoe and arm
band to remind him of his commitment to Christ.

Finally the day came when he was sent into a game.
He got a pitchout and ran off tackle for 6 yards. The next
play he scrambled for 32 yards. Following runs included
55-, 22-, 20- and 11-yard gains, and he led his team that
day in defeating Carolina 29–14. As he trotted off the
field, 86,000 fans went bananas as the announcer stated
that Archie's 239 yards for the day had broken the single-
game rushing record for Ohio State. On the sidelines he
dropped to his knees and lifted his index finger, indicating
not "Archie number 1" but "Jesus number 1."

With this as a start, he went on to become the first
sophomore to win the Big Ten Conference Most Valuable

Player award. He set an unbelievable mark for rushing 100 or more yards in 31 straight games. He smashed NCAA records with a cumulative 5,177-yard career.

How did "Butterball" become the "Cannonball" of the nation's top-ranked college football team? It was by deciding to annihilate anything that came between him and the goal line. His motto was "It's not the size of the dog in the fight that matters. It's the size of the fight in the dog!"

What kind of a fighter are you against the weeds in your life? Are you willing to let the Holy Spirit pull out those things that are displeasing to Him? Are you willing for God to develop you into the fighter He wants you to be? Are you tough enough to be different and live for God?

Putting it into my life
1. Define "weed" as it applies to your life.
2. Come up with an example of a "weed" in your life.
3. Write out a prayer asking the Lord to help you have the strength and determination to pull the "weed(s)" in your life.

W E E D

1

Rebellion

"Far be it from us to rebel against the Lord, and
turn away from him today" (Joshua 22:29a).

Crab grass is a pesky weed to have growing in your
yard. It starts with a few sprouts growing here and
there – almost unnoticed – but before long, its growth is
nearly uncontrollable. Its runners can rapidly cover a
yard, even climbing planters to choke out potted plants.
And, boy, is it hard to get rid of!

We could compare crab grass to rebellion in a life. It
often starts out small, but it can rapidly take over a life.

Chuck Swindoll, radio speaker, author and pastor, is a
friend to many of us. In his book, *Strengthening Your
Grip*, he said this about rebellion:

> Question Authority! These words are not simply a
> bumper sticker slogan found on vans in Southern
> California, they're fast becoming the unwritten motto
> of the 1980s. Let's face it, this generation is tough, not
> tender. No longer
>
> • is the voice of the parent respected in the home
> • is the sight of the policeman on the corner a model
> of courage and control
> • is the warning of the teacher in the classroom
> feared and obeyed

- is the reprimand of the boss sufficient to bring about change
- is the older person treated with dignity and honor
- is the husband considered the "head of the home" (God help him if he even thinks such a thing!)[1]

Rock star Tina Turner agrees. In a recent television interview she said this: "Everybody today is rebelling. It's part of our day." Many people may be rebelling—even Christians—but few recognize it for what it is—a destructive force!

When we think of "rebels" we might picture men in gray fatigues waving Dixie flags and singing "Oh, I wish I was in the land of cotton, old times there are not forgotten . . ." Perhaps you think of the Palestine Liberation Organization (PLO) in Lebanon. The Bible, however, shows us a rather different picture of a rebel. When it speaks of rebellion, it points back to rebellion's originator—Satan.

How you have fallen from heaven,
　O morning star, son of the dawn!
You have been cast down to the earth,
　you who once laid low the nations!
You said in your heart,
　"I will ascend to heaven;
I will raise my throne
　above the stars of God;
I will ascend above the tops of the clouds;
　I will make myself like the Most High." (Isaiah
　14:12–14)

What makes rebellion so bad? It is the exact pattern Satan followed when he went against God. Satan could not handle God's Lordship. In fact, he wanted to be God himself, so he tried removing God by rebelling against His order.

To put it simply, rebellion is a weed. And it must go! It can creep in and eventually cause us to go against God's standards for our lives. When we rebel, we are saying, "My idea is better than God's way."

My friend Jim discovered this the hard way. Jim had it all going for him. As a freshman in high school, he could bench press 250 pounds. He was handsome and well liked. He seldom had to study hard for tests. His parents were wealthy, and he had just about anything he wanted. He was a starting athlete at whatever sport he tried out for. Even with all of this going for him, Jim lacked one thing: a teachable attitude.

Jim argued constantly with his teachers and his parents. He became so mad one day after practice that he punched his coach several times, knocking him to the ground. That cost him 10 days' suspension from school and his team uniform.

At this point, Jim only became more rebellious. He refused to abide by any rules and despised all authority. This attitude even repelled his friends; none of them could stand his cocky, "don't-mess-with-me" attitude. The last I heard of Jim, he had been in jail twice. To this day, he is unable to see that *he* is the one with the problem.

As I talk with people who, like Jim, have a rebellious, unteachable spirit, I am reminded of another man I heard about. One day while he slept, someone put Limburger cheese on his mustache. When he awoke, he noticed a sour scent. He sniffed and said, "This couch stinks." As he got up, he could still smell something awful. He said,

"This room stinks." Becoming annoyed, he went into other parts of the house. No matter where he went, the horrible odor was there. Finally, he decided, "This whole house stinks!"

Wanting to get out of the house for some fresh air, he climbed into his car for a drive around the neighborhood. But the smell was still there. He then began to think that something must surely be wrong in the neighborhood, and it really began to bother him. As he drove frantically about, sniffing for relief and finding none, his final conclusion was, "THIS WHOLE WORLD STINKS!"

Jim was like that man. The problem was not with the rest of the world—it was with him; it was right under his nose. *He* needed to change. More than that he needed God to change him. He needed to incorporate God's plan of submission to authority into his life.

One night after youth group, Kim walked up to me. I could tell that she hadn't agreed with some of the things I had been sharing on this idea of submission. These were her comments: "It's not *that bad* to go against authority. After all, I'm 16. If I don't buck the system, I'll be some kind of weirdo. I've got to fight for my rights, you know. If I don't, my parents will think they can treat me like a doormat or something. You have to 'climb the ladder' by yourself. If you don't, you'll get run over."

I felt sorry for Kim. She had been ripped off. Someone had convinced her that rebelling was fighting for her rights. God says, "Don't believe it!" Some form of the word "rebel" appears in the Bible 96 times. Here are a few samples of what God thinks about rebels and rebellion:

For rebellion is like the sin of divination [witchcraft],

and arrogance like the evil of idolatry. (1 Samuel
15:22)

Many times he delivered them,
  but they were bent on rebellion
  and they wasted away in their sin. (Psalm 106:43)

Yet they rebelled
  and grieved his Holy Spirit.
So he turned and became their enemy
  and he himself fought against them. (Isaiah 63:10)

This kind of straightforwardness about rebellion is not
popular in our society. It cuts across the grain of the "I-
ain't-gonna-let-anyone-shove-me-around" attitude of today.
As I was discipling a teen by the name of Randy, I discovered a rebellious attitude in him: "No one runs me over! I
can make up my own mind, can't I? What is the big deal?"

"Randy," I said, "the big deal is that if you are going to
be your best for God, rebellion has got to go! You're right,
you do have the ability to make up your own mind. God
respects your freedom and wants you to freely choose His
will. But the longer you wait to pull that weed, the
deeper the roots go."

The life of Solomon is an excellent illustration of the
danger of rebellion. In First Kings 9:1–7, God told Solomon that if he honored the Lord in his life, He would bless
him as He had blessed no other man. If rebellion were
allowed, however, disaster was sure to follow. Unfortunately, Solomon did not listen to God. He gradually per-
mitted idol worship in the temple. His convictions began
to slip until he no longer was offended by sin. As a result,
affliction and frustration were his companions. Enemies

came from all over to harass him. Age crept upon him rapidly, and as time ran out, there were no longer any delights in living. Rebellion had stolen the best from Solomon.

Do you see the pattern? Solomon's life of rebellion was not a "one minute he was serving the Lord, and the next he turned away" situation. Instead, it was a progressive decline. It was erosion—one inch at a time—until finally there was no foundation in his life.

How about you?

Does God want to do something in your life, but maybe because you aren't submissive, He can't? Only He knows the potential that could be unleased if you would just let Him have His way.

How do you become submissive? Learn to say yes to the Lord. Start by being submissive to the God-placed authorities in your life. By doing that, you are saying yes to God. It works like this:

- If your parents ask you to cut the grass, God is asking you to cut the grass.
- If your boss asks you to work harder or to be punctual, God is asking you to work harder or to be punctual.
- If your teacher says, "For homework tonight, I want you to . . . ," God is saying, "For homework tonight, I want you to . . ."
- If the speed limit says 45 mph, God says 45 mph.

The only time you should not be in complete obedience to those in authority over you is when that authority violates God's Word.

Has crab grass—rebellion—overrun your garden? Maybe the idea of "Question Authority" promoted by this generation has its roots in you now. If so, why not give this "clenched fist" attitude a dropkick. Daniel 9:5–6 helps us to see rebellion for all that it is: "We have sinned and done wrong. We have been wicked and have rebelled; we have turned away from your commands and laws." The Lord will honor you for being honest and willing to change your attitude. Daniel 9:9 tells us, "The Lord our God is merciful and forgiving, even though we have rebelled against him."

Why not begin pulling the weed of rebellion today? As you yank it up strand by strand, you will once again discover what true freedom is all about. The key to such freedom is in your submission to the God-ordered authorities in your life.

Putting it into my life
1. Why is crab grass compared to rebellion?
2. List some of society's attitudes toward authority.
3. Who are some authorities in your life?
4. If the Lord brings to your mind any person against whom you have rebelled, go to that person and ask for forgiveness.

WEED 2
Peer Pressure

"It was for freedom that Christ set us free. Stand
firm, then, and do not let yourselves be
burdened again by a yoke of slavery"
(Galatians 5:1).

When nettles begin to break through the ground as
a new plant, they are attractive. The would-be
gardener may be encouraged by the sight of their bright
green leaves. This joy is short-lived, however, because
nettles are weeds. The burning itch caused by contact
with their leaves is difficult to relieve.

Nettles can be put to good use, though. Some people
plant them around gardens to act as a hedge or a fence.
They help to keep out rabbits and other varmints.

So nettles can be harmful and helpful.

Peer pressure is like that. It can steal life and inflict
pain to those who get caught in it. But it can also act as a
hedge, guarding teens from mistakes that can damage and
even ruin their lives.

Actually, peer pressure can affect us in three ways:

1. It can be a good influence.
2. It can be a bad influence.
3. It can be neutral—not really bad, but not really good
   either.

As we work through this, see where you fit in.

It is possible to be influenced by people who are not really bad but who are not really good either. Let me illustrate. When I was in high school, we had jello every Thursday. About 30 guys would gather around a table in the cafeteria for the weekly competition of "jello-sucking." To win, you had to inhale the largest portion of jello in one breath. As the stuff slithered down our throats like raw oysters, there were various comments: "Look at vacuum-cleaner lips go!" or "You guys are really gross." This wasn't a bad influence, but it wasn't a great one either.

Fortunately, we all know someone who is a good influence on our lives. It may be an uncle, a parent, a cousin, a coach, a teacher, a brother or sister or a friend. We all have someone like this whom we admire.

Alice found she had some helpful friends. Alice had a problem with her temper. To put it bluntly, she was "bullheaded" and even mean at times. She hated these things in her life and genuinely wanted to be different. While at a retreat one summer, she sensed the Lord speaking to her about her temper. Several of her close friends prayed with her about her attitude. God used these friends as a good influence in Alice's life that week. So, in this instance, peer pressure was helpful.

Being a teenager and a positive, godly influence on your friends is not easy. The pressure to swear, tell bad jokes and be sexually active is powerful. It has smothered many teens. Coping with this kind of pressure is a tough fight, and the opponents have often delivered knock-out punches. This past summer, I heard about just such an incident.

A group of kids were bored one Friday night, so they

thought they would have some fun. With a particular country road outside of town in mind, they devised a prank. They covered the center line on the road with dirt and painted a fake center line that veered off in the opposite direction. Then they hid by the side of the road to see what would happen.

It was a foggy night, and a school bus bringing the ball team home from an out-of-town game came down the road. The bus driver was not familiar with the road, so when he came to the part "adjusted" by these teens, he followed the new markings. The bus went off the road and plunged over a cliff, killing the entire team.

It is hard to admit to having bad influences in our lives, and it takes guts to be different. Fred had the guts. Unfortunately, Sara did not. Here are their stories:

Fred's story: I was watching horror movies at Howard's house, as I often did on Saturday nights, when, during one of the commercials, Howard went over to check the door to make sure his parents weren't around. Then he got a strange smirk on his face and said, "I went to bed with a girl the other night."

I was munching on popcorn, so I pretended I had choked on a kernel. This was a topic I was not used to talking about, and I didn't know what to say, so I said nothing. I just watched the commercial and ate popcorn.

After a few moments, Howard mocked, "What's wrong with you? Haven't you ever taken a girl to bed before? Everyone is doing it."

As long as he was pressing me on it, I figured there was no choice but to respond. "No, Howard, I don't intend to take a girl to bed until she is my wife, and then I am sure it will be fantastic!"

At that point I think he called me a few names like Prude or Straight or Holy Joe. It didn't bother me at the time, because Howard was the first of my friends to go off and have premarital sex. He seemed, at the time, to be the oddball. But, later, after several more of my close friends started, I was in the minority. The tide changed and started to move against me, and I was often tempted to give in to the way "everybody else" was living. I am glad I never did.[2]

Sara's story: Sara is a girl in our youth group. She is very pretty, has a great personality and, with some work, could be a top-notch musician. She came to me after Bible study concerned about a friend. As she talked to me about Danny, I gathered he was a great guy. She wasn't sure, however, if he was a Christian and had not talked to him about this. Sara wanted to talk to Danny about Jesus, but the problem was that she was afraid of what people would think of her. She didn't want to be thought of as being "different."

The peer pressure Sara was facing was putting her into a mold formed by *others*. The worst part is this: those same people are strapped into the same mold. It is not hard to get caught in the trap. Before you know it, you are just like everyone else: same jeans, same T-shirts, same food, same music, same thoughts—same old junk.

Of the three influences (positive, neutral, negative), which one affects you?

22

What does the Lord say?

During one of our youth group meetings, we talked about some of these things. One teen, Jennifer, said to me: "Les, does the Lord really care about all this? After all, I don't see how being a 'freak' is honoring the Lord. I don't think we should be on some sort of 'free-from-reality flight.'"

Neither do I. God doesn't call teens to be weird, but He does call them to be liberated from negative peer pressure and to be liberators for others.

The thief comes only to steal and kill and destroy; I have come that they may have life, and have it to the full. (John 10:10)

Where the Spirit of the Lord is, there is freedom. (2 Corinthians 3:17)

Dr. James Dobson, the well-known Christian psychologist, has done extensive research in the area of peer pressure. Here's what he has to say:

This pressure to conform is at its worst during adolescence. . . . A team of doctors decided to conduct an experiment to study the ways in which this kind of group pressure influences young people. To accomplish this they invited 10 young people into a room and told them they were going to evaluate their perception in order to learn how well each student could see the front of the room from where he sat. But just between us, all of the teenagers were very close to the front of the room and everybody could see quite easily. What the doctors were actually studying was not the students' eyesight, but the effects of this kind of pressure. So the doctors said: "We're going to hold up some cards at the front of the room, and on each card are three lines: line A, line B and line C. Each will be a different length. In some cases, line A will be the longest; in some cases line B will be the longest; and in still other cases line C will be the longest. Several dozen cards will be shown in a different order. Now we will hold them up and point to line A, B and C on each card. When we point to the longest line, please raise your hand to show that you know that it is longer than the others." So they repeated their directions to make sure everyone understood. . . . Then they raised one card and pointed to the top line.

What one student didn't know was that the other nine had been secretly informed earlier to vote not for the longest line but the second longest line. . . . So when the doctors held up the first card and pointed to line A, which was clearly shorter than line B, all nine students cooperated in this scheme and raised their hands. The fellow being studied didn't know that the other nine were in on the joke, and he looked around in disbelief. It was obvious that line A was shorter than line B, but everyone seemed to think it was longer. Later he admitted thinking: "Boy, I must not have been listening to the directions. Somehow I missed the point, and I'd better do what everyone else is doing or they'll laugh at me." So he carefully raised his hand with the rest of the group. The researchers explained again. Then they held up the second card, and again nine people voted for the wrong line, and the confused fellow became even more tense over this predicament. But he eventually raised his hand with the group once more. Over and over again he voted *with* the group, even though he *knew* they were wrong. This young man was not unusual. In fact, more than 75 percent of the young people who were tested behaved in the same way. . . . They simply didn't have the courage to say: "The group is wrong. I can't explain why, but you guys are all confused." And this is what group pressure does.[3]

Maybe you're thinking to yourself: "WOW! You almost have to be from Mars to avoid getting caught in the trap of peer pressure. I don't think I can handle this stuff!" As I said earlier, it takes guts to be different and not get creamed by negative peer pressure. Granted the price is high, but it is worth it.

Here's another example of a teen determined to pay that price. And what a difference he made! As a teen, Sam faced all the temptations that normal teens face. It seemed every day his friends would challenge him: "Come on, Sam! If you are going to be a 'real man' you've got to get the ladies. We'll show you how it's done." Or: "Look Sammy ol' boy, if you're going to be cool today, you've got to drop this 'honoring the Lord' business. Get aggressive, man. Learn to cheat! Everyone does it. If you don't, you'll lose." Or: "Hey Sam, wanna party? Oh, yeah, we forgot, you love God more than 'fun'."

Despite the pressure, Sam refused to get caught up in what everybody else was doing. His goal was to serve God with all of his heart. And look what the Bible says about our man: "The Lord was with Samuel as he grew up, and he let none of his words fall to the ground" (1 Samuel 3:19).

Samuel was a pacesetter in his day; he refused to succumb to peer pressure. You can be a pacesetter, too, but it demands paying the price. Are you willing?

Dena is a pacesetter. She was introduced to my wife, Kay, and me when we lived in Pennsylvania. Right away we could tell she was a leader. She was involved in majorettes, had a job at a grocery store as a cashier, was attractive and had a steady boyfriend. She attended public school, and experienced all the temptations of peer pressure. In all of that, she maintained her walk with Jesus. She attends a university now, where living for Christ can be difficult. She has made that her choice, however, and isn't going to back down. Her goal is to be a pacesetter for God in spite of peer pressure.

How do the Denas and Samuels make it against the fierce struggle of peer pressure? Do they ever get tired of the fight? Do they ever yell at the top of their lungs: "FORGET IT, GOD! I CAN'T TAKE IT ANYMORE"?

Sure they get discouraged and want to quit. But a pacesetter doesn't quit. Why? Because a winner never quits, and a quitter never wins! Any dead fish can float downstream. The challenge is to be a fighter against the tide of peer pressure!

What about you?

The ball is in your court. What kind of a person will you be? Will you settle for being like those young people Dr. Dobson talked about? Will you just "go with the flow"? Or will you determine to set the course of your journey upstream?

Uprooting the weed of negative peer pressure is a tough job. But with God's help, you can break out of the trap. You have a choice. You can be miserable in trying to be like everybody else, or you can be free.

And is it ever great to be free! Remember Sara? She got tired of society's expectations. She has recently been set free. As I am sitting in my living room wrapping up this chapter, I just received a call. Sara started Bible college four days ago. She has decided to be a pacesetter. Praise the Lord!

This world could use a few more Denas and Samuels and Freds and Saras. Will you join their ranks?

Putting it into my life

1. Why are nettles compared to peer pressure?
2. Make a list of people who have influenced your life. Now categorize them into the three areas we have discussed: good, neutral and bad.
3. Write out why you have allowed them to influence your life.
4. Ask yourself: "Are they worth the privilege of being in my life?"

W E E D 3

Thought Life

"For as [a man] thinks within himself, so he is"
(Proverbs 23:7, NASB).

Dandelions are another troublesome weed. After the yellow flower dries, it becomes a round, puffy container that is full of seeds. When this head is kicked or mowed over, the seeds are blown by the wind. Wherever the seeds land, they begin a new plant. They can spread throughout a whole yard almost overnight. In fact, dandelions can become a problem for an entire neighborhood. And once they take root, they are difficult to get rid of.

Evil thoughts are similar to dandelions. Once they take root, their seeds can spread over our whole thought life. Soon they are controlling us. It has been said, "You are what you eat." Let's change one word: "You are what you *think*." And, as American author Ralph Waldo Emerson said, "You are what you think *all day long*!" Our opening verse goes right to the point: "For as [a man] thinks within himself, so he is."

What is your thought life like? What's on your mind most of the time? Imagine having your thoughts somehow recorded on a video tape and shown to your school's entire student body at an assembly. Would it be embarrassing?

I want to be honest with you. When I was in high

school, I was controlled by evil thoughts. Lust, passion, greed and jealousy consumed me. Godly convictions and standards were gradually being choked out by this weed, as its seeds took root in my life. Similar to trying to control dandelions, ridding my mind of evil thoughts appeared to be a losing battle. No matter how hard I tried, the weed of evil thoughts proved to be too powerful for me to overcome.

My friend John had the same problem. John was a strong Christian when we started high school together. He had received Christ as his Savior in the seventh grade. Soon he was sharing Jesus with others. He even started a Bible study on an open lot where kids met to play football after school. He junked his rock-and-roll T-shirts and burned his record collection. He ignored the "cheap shots" taken at him for being so zealous for the Lord. Of the 1,700 kids in our high school, John was the only one I can recall who prayed before he ate his lunch in the cafeteria.

When we started the 10th grade, however, John began to cool down in his commitment to Christ. He mentioned how he struggled with his thought life and how, secretly, he spent time thinking of ways to talk his girlfriend into having sex with him. He enjoyed letting his mind wander at the beach as the girls strolled by in their tiny bikinis. He began to think that maybe he *was* missing out on all the fun at the weekend parties people talked about on Monday in class.

As this stuff wove itself into John's thought life, he began missing youth activities at the church. Before long his vocabulary was different. He used curse words with apparently no sting of conscience. By Christmas of that year, he was smoking pot, skipping school and causing trouble for his parents. The kids he once tried to win to Christ no longer saw him as a threat. Tragically, within a year, he dropped out of school completely and drifted into life—a frustrated, misguided young man.

How do kids who were once "spark plugs" in their youth groups and in their schools end up as "duds"? I am convinced that this process of erosion begins in the thought life. Failure to pull this weed right away guarantees a one-way ticket to the loser's corner.

Because an undesirable thought life can knock out even the toughest teen, some plans are needed to counteract its attack. One of the best strategies is to ask questions and to know the patterns of the opponent. As we move along, be ready for some answers on how to control and deal with an evil thought life.

Do evil thoughts come to everyone, or am I weird?

Of all the 5 billion people who share planet earth, not one is exempt from thinking evil thoughts. The Apostle Paul wasn't even exempt. Look at what he says in Romans 7:

> So I find this law at work: When I want to go good, evil is right there with me. For in my inner being I delight in God's law; but I see another law at work in the members of my body, waging war against the law of my mind and making me a prisoner of the law of sin at work within my members. What a wretched man I am! Who will rescue me from this body of death? Thanks be to God—through Jesus Christ our Lord! (verses 21–25)

Did you get that? The man who started many churches, who preached the gospel over much of the Mediterranean, who was used in a healing ministry, who was called *the* apostle of apostles and who was the one the Lord used to write half the New Testament! This same man admits he struggled with his thought life. So you and I are not alone.

Where do evil thoughts originate?

The answer: Satan! Although we don't physically see Satan as the little red man with a pointed tail, horns on his head and a pitchfork in his hand, he is the one with whom we do battle. And when he attacks, it's usually in our thought life. He is the one who plants those bad thoughts in our minds. Just look at this:

> Put on the full armor of God so that you can take your stand against the devil's schemes [schemes mean the deception of evil thoughts]. (Ephesians 6:11)

The devil knows if we cultivate the seed he plants in our minds, we are on our way into a tailspin in our Christian walk.

Can I ever be completely free from Satan's initial attacks in my thought life?

There is no one who can hand you a formula guaranteeing total freedom from the possibility of having evil thoughts. Even Jesus had them hurled at Him. Luke 4:13 says, "When the devil had finished all this tempting, he left him until an opportune time." As long as we live, evil thoughts will come our way. Satan will see to that, just as he did with Jesus.

When I shared this with my friend Bill, he gave me a puzzled look. He understood that Satan attacks everyone and plants the initial seed in his or her mind. Yet he brought up this question:

"Then why am I guilty?"

We are not guilty for having the bad thoughts presented to us—in the same way that Jesus was not guilty when Satan tempted Him. Dwelling on evil thoughts is what causes the problems. When we do that, evil thoughts become weeds in our life.

Have your ever thought about—

- cheating?
- getting drunk to help you forget about certain situations?
- acting out the words to songs on secular rock albums?
- seeing a girl naked on the beach?
- owning a pair of X-ray glasses?

Satan cannot make us spend time thinking about these things. We elect to do that on our own—and when we do, *we are guilty!* The worst part of this is that the longer we choose to dwell on these things, the more fertilizer we apply to the growing weeds of evil thoughts.

Fill 'em up

Our thought life is like the gas we put into a car. If you put in cheap gas, you get cheap performance. I remember my first car—it was a Mercury Cougar. The night before I got it, I was so excited I could hardly sleep. Finally the next day, after all the legal work was cared for, I drove over to my friend's house to show him my new "chariot." I pulled into Mike's driveway, blew the horn and he came out, climbed in and off we went down the boulevard.

As we were cruising along listening to the Top Ten records of that week, I thought I'd be cool and show him how I could blow the doors off any car on the street. I stepped on the gas pedal with all my might. (In looking back I am surprised that I didn't put a hole right through the floorboard!) Fully expecting to take off like the Space Shuttle, I suddenly came back to earth as I heard an awful clattering and pinging sound coming from the engine. I was so embarrassed and humiliated that I sort of wilted right behind the steering wheel. I was sure that I had just bought a piece of junk. Later I found out that the problem was the fuel I had put in the car. The octane was not high enough; therefore, the engine couldn't run at top performance.

Think for a moment—what do you put into the fuel tank of your mind? What about the jokes you tell? What are your favorite records saying to you? What goes into your head via your reading material? Are rock stars the "superstars" in your life? Do you struggle with envy over the guy or gal who is better looking and seems to attract the most popular dates? Do you want something so bad that you think of ways of stealing it? Is your dating life so lonely that you have considered lowering your standards? If you have struggled in some of these areas, you *can* be released.

Clearing the ground for grass and flowers
You are no doubt saying, "I've heard all this before. I know my thought life stinks, and I am concerned. Yet I find myself thinking the same old, junky, trashy thoughts. As a

matter of fact, it keeps getting worse. I guess there is no hope for me, because the only thing I know about winning over evil thoughts is defeat."

If this describes you, here are some answers:

Get a Bible you can understand and read it! It is God's number one "weed-killer." Why? Look at what Jesus did when Satan tempted Him. What was His response? "It is written . . ." "It is written . . ." "It is written . . ." The next time your thought life gets off balance, try using one of the following of God's "weed-killers:"

> Finally, brothers, whatever is true, whatever is noble, whatever is right, whatever is pure, whatever is lovely, whatever is admirable, whatever is excellent or praiseworthy – think about such things. (Philippians 4:8)

> You will keep in perfect peace him whose mind is steadfast, because he trusts in you. (Isaiah 26:3)

> Set your minds on things above, not on earthly things. (Colossians 3:2)

> But we have the mind of Christ. (1 Corinthians 2:16b)

> We demolish arguments and every pretension that sets itself up against the knowledge of God, and we take captive every thought to make it obedient to Christ. (2 Corinthians 10:5)

Refuse to dwell on thoughts that are ungodly. We all have thoughts that could drag us down if we dwelt on them. But if we replace them as soon as they arrive and don't give them room to grow, they won't grow. Martin Luther, a man used of God to change his world in the 1500s, said this about allowing evil thoughts to hang around too long: "You cannot keep the birds from flying over your head, but you do not have to let them build a nest in your hair!"

Not long after Janet became a Christian, she decided she wanted victory over her thought life. It seemed that at the exact moment when she felt the most confident about her spiritual life, Bang! Evil thoughts would start popping into her head. So she started using Scripture as a weapon against these thoughts. Janet is convinced that had she not done this, she would have many "birds' nests in her hair."

Ask Christ for His thoughts. Bill Weston is an evangelist with Youth for Christ. A remarkable youth speaker, he says this about asking Christ for His thoughts: "I ask Jesus every day for His thoughts. I pray, 'Lord, fill my brains with things that I wouldn't be afraid to ask You to bless. If You don't, I'll fall flat on my face, and that won't honor You. Thank You, Jesus." If Bill Weston, who has been a minister for 40 years, needs to ask Christ for godly thoughts, don't we?

Stretch your mind. Our minds sleep if we let them. We need to engage them—especially with the things of God. I read Christian books. This keeps my mind from wandering and relieves boredom when, for instance, I am waiting at the dentist's office or some other place. Another good idea is to carry Scripture cards or listen to Christian music.

On to the winner's circle

We have seen in this chapter that evil thoughts can be like dandelions—they can consume our entire person. We have also seen that we don't have to let this happen. With the ammunition of Scripture, the refusal to give ungodly thoughts room to develop, the mind of Christ and the correct engagement of our minds, we can fight and win against evil thoughts. God is looking for teenagers who will take His challenge to be different in their thinking. Is He calling you?

Not long ago I found the following that illustrates how our thoughts affect our actions. Look at the connection: THOUGHTS – ACTS – HABITS – CHARACTER – DESTINY! It is clear: our thoughts control how we live. That is why we need to have thoughts that are true and honorable before God. By going God's way in your thought life, you will be the *victor*. The one who doesn't will be the *victim*.

Putting it into my life

1. Why are dandelions compared to evil thoughts?
2. What influences your thinking the most? the second most?
3. How do these things match up against Scripture?
4. Make a list of ways that you can put pure thoughts into your "thinking tank." Start using this list today.

W E E D

4

Your Past

"Come to me, all you who are weary and
burdened, and I will give you rest"
(Matthew 11:28).

Kudzu is a weed that, once planted, tends to cover large areas of land quickly. It climbs over bushes, hedges and even the tallest of trees, blocking out the sun. It has thick leaves and vines that can be literally miles long. Kudzu has been known to choke out entire forests.

Our past life can be likened to kudzu. The thick leaves of yesterday's mistakes can wrap around us, shutting out the rays of God's will for our lives.

As a pastor on a college campus, I frequently talk with young people struggling with their past. I have heard them say things like:

"If only I had not done _____."
"That was so stupid! I knew better!"
"There is no way God could love me after what I did."
"When God thinks of me, He probably throws up."

If you feel that way or know of someone who does, there's great news—Jesus enjoys setting people free from their past mistakes and sins.

Understanding problems from the past
When people talk negatively about their pasts, they usu-

ally mention it in one of three categories: mistakes, child abuse or past sins. Let's look at these different categories and see what God has to say about each.

Mistakes

Mistakes come in all sizes and shapes. They can be embarrassing, such as the time Ruth walked into the boys' dressing room while they were showering after baseball practice.

Mistakes can also be funny. Pam and Steve tell this story about their wedding. They had set their wedding date at a time that conflicted with the plans of a favorite uncle. Although he was unable to attend, he sent a telegram of best wishes to the new couple. At the bottom of the telegram was the reference of First John 4:18. That is where the trouble began.

Apparently there was a misunderstanding in the telegraph office, because when the note arrived, instead of First John 4:18, it had John 4:18. Can you imagine the surprise the newlyweds received when they read this reference: "For you have had five husbands, and the one whom you now have is not your husband."

This kind of mistake does not cause real problems, though. Others, however, can be tragic. This was true for John.

John and Gary were best friends while growing up. They played football in junior and senior high school together. They saw each other when they were home for breaks from their separate colleges. They were each other's best man at their weddings.

They had always dreamed of going to Wyoming to hunt elk. Finally, they were able to work out vacation time together. They saved their money and bought equipment for the trip. It was going to be great.

On the second day out, there was a tragic mishap. John and Gary became separated. John heard a rustling in the bushes. Without thinking, he pointed his gun and fired. He heard a thud and ran into the brush where he found Gary dead.

Facing mistakes

Mistakes may be choking you off from reaching your potential for God. Possibly, as you are reading this chapter, you are thinking: "I don't want to talk about it. I can't do anything right. I am a failure! God can't work with me. Face it! I'm a failure."

You are not alone in thinking that way. I am sure that when

- Mark Spitz first tried to swim he almost drowned
- Babe Ruth had struck out 1,330 times, he felt like a jerk
- John Casey received his 753rd rejection letter he was ready to quit (he went on to write 564 books)
- Abraham Lincoln lost in his 17th attempt to be elected to public office, he thought, "What's the use?"
- Bobby Kennedy failed the third grade and failed at managing a paper route, he felt like a complete failure
- Ed Gibson, one of the astronauts on the Skylab III mission, failed first and fourth grades, he was unhappy

But each one went on and succeeded. You can, too, because God's acceptance is not given according to accomplishments. He loves us no matter how large our goof-ups are.

Child abuse

Today we hear a great deal about child abuse. A *USA Today* report (May 28, 1987) said that

- in 1984 1.7 million cases of child abuse were reported
- in 86 percent of the cases, abuse was inflicted by the parent
- one in 4 girls and one in 10 boys under 18 will be involved in some form of forced sexual experience with an adult

Being abused as a child is something that haunts many people. Whether it is done physically, emotionally or verbally, it always wounds and scars. That was the way it was for Amy.

Amy was raped by a landlord when she was 10. She had gone camping with his family for the weekend. While the others were at the showers, he had her come into the camper. There he abused her and demanded that she tell no one.

As she sat in my office and expressed her hurt and betrayal, tears flowed like a river. She had kept her experience to herself for 12 years. Her comments were something like this: "The hardest thing about this is that my trust and innocent love were betrayed."

If an incident of this nature is in your past, or if you know of someone else who has been abused as a child, please give attention to the following:

A. Tell someone. It is okay to tell. You are not weird, and there is someone who can help you.
B. Look to God for recovery. Ask questions and vent your frustrations. Don't be afraid. He is there with relief.

First Peter 5:7 says, "Cast all your anxiety on him because he cares for you."

C. Read. I recommend the following books: *Healing for Damaged Emotions* and *Healing of Memories* by David Seamands and *His Image . . . My Image* by Josh McDowell. They offer real help for people who struggle with memories of child abuse. This is a starting place for these delicate situations.

There is help for the hurting, and Jesus will carry you through.

Past sins

Along with mistakes and child abuse there is also the problem of past sins. Past sins cause pain for many teens. And guilt and fear of what God must be thinking keep them from addressing the problem.

Ken felt like this. As we were walking home from shooting basketball, I noticed a strange look in his eye. Gradually he opened up to me about an incident in his life. He had found a wallet on the side of the road. Inside the wallet was a VISA card. He took the card to a nearby mall and bought $700 worth of tires, stereos, clothes and sports equipment. He told me how for almost a year now, he had been "looking over his shoulder" because he felt so guilty. He was sure that the Lord was going to "zap" him with a bolt of lightning at any time.

I wish you could have seen Ken's face after I showed him the following verses. He lit up as he saw God's reaction to people who want to repent of something from their past.

If we confess our sins, he is faithful and just and will

forgive us our sins and purify us from all unrighteous-ness. (1 John 1:9)

He prays to God and finds favor with him,
    he sees God's face and shouts for joy;
    he is restored by God to his righteous state. (Job
        33:26)

Ken was overjoyed. He prayed and asked God to for-give him. The last I heard, he had contacted the person to whom the VISA card belonged and was mowing lawns to pay for the stuff he bought illegally. The best part of it all was that he was enjoying the freedom Jesus gave him.

God can do that for you, too, no matter what has happened in your past. God's grace is sufficient to cover your sin, if you truly repent and ask Him to forgive you. Ken found that out, and so did John.

John grew up hearing about Jesus, but he did not believe what he heard. He had always dreamed of being a sailor and of having a woman in every port. He wanted to live a wild life without any restrictions. He thought the Christian life was for the "mamma's boy," and that was the last thing he was interested in.

John left home in his early teens, pursuing life just as he had planned—fast, free and dangerous. Soon he be-came involved in adultery. He was also a racketeer in slavery. He had even murdered—all by the age of 16.

As the years passed, John began to think about his life. He felt guilty and dirty and, worst of all, he was afraid. He began to think about the message he had heard when he was young—that Jesus would forgive and cleanse anyone who would call out to Him. Was it possible that he might have this forgiveness?

One day John could stand it no longer. He got down on his knees and wept like a baby, confessing his past sins to God. As he prayed, God flooded his heart with a peace and a joy that he had never known before. It was as if he was a new person. He was completely pardoned!

John found out that Jesus had the real answers. Living a life dedicated to God was what real living was all about. He began telling his friends about Jesus and the change that had taken place in his life. He is still doing that today through his music. You've heard it before, for the song John Newton wrote was this:

Amazing Grace, how sweet the sound
   that saved a wretch like me.
I once was lost, but now am found,
   was blind but now I see.

What is in your past? Is it full of mistakes, hurts and past sins? Jesus can pull it all together if you will ask Him to. He can clear away the kudzu of your past. You don't have to make your life "presentable" before you turn to God. In fact, you couldn't do it if you wanted to. God simply says, "Let me put all the broken and missing pieces of your life together. You don't have to be afraid. I love you and have great things ahead for you."

Will you do that now? Ask God to root out the kudzu that keeps you enslaved. He loves to set people free.

Putting it into my life
1. Why is kudzu compared to our past lives?
2. What is the hardest thing for you to deal with about your past?

3. Will you ask the Lord to begin to change some things in your life now and to let the healing come?
4. Write out a prayer. Be honest and specific. As you turn your situation over to the Lord, watch how He makes some things come together for you, perhaps for the first time in your life.

5

W E D

Good Times Only

"Making the most of every opportunity, because
the days are evil" (Ephesians 5:16).

Clover is an inconspicuous weed. It can be beneficial. Bees use it to make honey; farmers feed it to their livestock. Usually, it grows in the shade where the ground is moist, because its shallow root system would quickly burn up in the scorching sun. While we can agree that clover is useful, most of us don't want clover growing in our front yards. Not only does it look bad, clover can choke out the grass.

Good times are like clover. They help us lead happy, fulfilled lives. But if we live our lives only for the good times, we can expect trouble.

Dave lived down the block from me when we were kids. Everyone liked him because he could always think of more ways to have fun than anyone I've ever met. One night, however, his plans backfired. Dave decided to have a camp-out in his backyard. His plan was to have everyone sneak down to the cement factory after midnight and play in the giant sandpiles. How cool an idea could you want? Right? Wrong—especially when the police caught us and took us back home to our parents at 2:00 o'clock in the morning! After this incident, Dave lost his "Good-time Charlie" position in the neighborhood.

I *love* to have fun. If there's a party or a celebration or a game, I want to be part of it. At our house, none of us goes to bed unless we have laughed, been tickled and had a winner of our daily "See who can be the biggest coconut head of the family today" contest. It is quite a competition for us. *Everyone* wants to win.

Even our extended family gets involved in playing the game. I suppose the all-time winner would have to be when our family was on vacation this past summer. Someone from our "kooky clan" walked up to a complete stranger on the beach and started talking with him. By the time the conversation was over, the stranger had been talked into going to the rest of the family and claiming to be someone famous. The stranger did this, totally amazing the rest of the family, while the instigator broke out in laughter.

Along with fun, though, there needs to be seriousness. The key word here is balance. Here is a story that illustrates this:

Some time ago, there was a group of potato farmers. For years their practice was to sell or keep only the best and the biggest potatoes from their crop. The smaller potatoes were used for seed for the next year's crop. Over the course of many years, they made a startling discovery: their potatoes had become the size of marbles! It became glaringly apparent to those farmers that they could not enjoy only the best that life has to offer and leave the rest for leftovers. The harvest reflected the planting.

Today the popular thought is this: the less work the

better. It's sort of a joke to hear, "When the going gets tough, the tough get going." Many teens think, "Tough? Who in the world wants to be tough? That means hard work and discipline. Let's just have a blast in life. After all, you only live once."

Larry was lazy. I often asked him why he didn't get serious about life. He responded, "I have serious thoughts, but when those things flash through my brain, I just roll over, pull up the sheets, close my eyes and after a while they go away." What a bore!

Good times only? Sounds great! We would all like to find the key that unlocks the door to the amusement park of life. There we could have a life filled with spine-tingling excitement. But we all know that there is more to life than good times and spine-tingling excitement. There are tough knocks, bruises and hard times. It is more than just being happy and planning the next fun event. Cartoonist Ralph Barton's tragic death illustrates a life that lacked balance.

Barton was one of the nation's top cartoonists. One day this note was left pinned to his pillow: "I have had few difficulties, many friends, great successes; I have gone from wife to wife and from house to house and visited countries of the world, but I am fed up with inventing devices to fill up 24 hours a day." Those are strong words from a man who was noted for making America smile as they read his comic strips in the morning paper. Apparently his life of fun wasn't really such fun after all.

Here is a list of things that are a part of many teens' lives. Write beside each one whether it is Very Important, Important or Not Very Important in your life.

Friends
Music
Television
Witnessing for Christ
Hobbies
Getting my class ring
Making the cheerleading team
Helping the hurting
Nice clothes
Parents
Education
Sports
Devotions
Owning my own car
Worship
Family time
Having a date every weekend
Popularity
Scripture memorization

Evaluating priorities

After prioritizing the list, ask yourself these two questions: "What is important to me?" "What is important to God?" Listen to what God says is important to Him: "But seek first [my] kingdom and [my] righteousness, and all these things will be given to you as well" (Matthew 6:33).

Tyler is tall, good looking and has a pleasing personality. He plays football for his high school team and runs track. But best of all, he knows what is really important.

Not long ago I asked him if he would like to go to the park with me and my family for the day. He said he would think about about it and let me know. When he called with his reply, the conversation went something like this: "Hi, Les. I appreciate your asking me to go with your family this weekend, but I can't make it. I haven't been at home much lately, and I need to be with *my* family. Thanks just the same, though." A decision like that says that Tyler is keeping a close eye out for any clover that may be popping up in his life!

God is looking for teens who will think about discipline. Usually when I say that to a group of teens, facial expressions respond back, "What a drag! God is against jokes, hates laughter and thinks it's a sin to have fun." That's not God's idea at all. He wants us to be happy. But He is looking for lives where discipline and fun are in balance.

Balance

While on a trip through Orlando, Florida, I stopped by a cemetery to visit the grave of a close friend. In the fall of 1977, a girl whom I had been dating was driving her Volkswagen when it was struck broadside by a tractor trailer. She was killed in the accident. Three days after her death, a dam broke at the college I attended, and the resulting flood killed 39 people. Seeing my friend's grave and remembering those who lost their lives in the flood caused me to stop and think. What really matters in life?

When we stand before God on judgment day, He isn't going to ask us how many dances we went to or how many miles we peddled our 10-speed bicycle. Rather, He will ask each of us questions like—

• What have you done that is of eternal value?
• What have you done for the kingdom of Christ?

- How did you use the abilities I gave you?
- Did you help the hurting?
- Explain to me how you gave My Word out to others.

If all we have to say is, "Well, uh, Lord, uh, I hit a few home runs for the church softball team," or "I made the ice cream cake for Mary's party in the sixth grade," or "I handed out Thanksgiving baskets once for the French club," or "I kept the nursery at church for the ladies' meeting," it is going to be a sad day. Being balanced in your life and serving Christ goes beyond just parties and fellowships and hurrah celebrations. It is a concerted effort to do something about people needing Jesus, people who will be lost unless they receive Him.

Sheri and JoAnne are both 17, juniors in high school, attractive and well liked. Sheri has won every award possible in high school volleyball; JoAnne works as a computer programmer after school. But do you know something else about these two girls? Both feel called to go to the mission field. They have adjusted their high school schedules so that they can graduate early and enroll in a Bible college. Their attitude is this: the sooner they get through college, the sooner they can get to the mission field. *That* is a balanced life with priorities that match the heart of God.

What's important to you? Do you enjoy lying in the clover field of good times and forgetting about the serious stuff? Are your priorities balanced? Look over the list again. Are you really balanced?

This chapter has been designed to make you think about what's really important, to make you think about the "size of the potatoes" you are planting for the next year, for the next decade and for eternity. "For eternity?" you might be saying; "I'm too young to think about eternity—even about 10 years from now."

The Bible talks about how God sees time. Because He is eternal, time doesn't govern Him. But because we are not eternal, time does govern us; we only have a few years in which to accomplish what God wants us to accomplish. What God wants us to see is that we need to live our lives so that they will count for eternity.

The Bible tells us that man's life span is about 70 years (Psalm 90:10) and that a thousand years of our time is like one day to God (2 Peter 3:8). I wondered what the ratio of the two would be, so I called Bernie, our youth group's whiz-kid, and asked him to figure it out on his computer. He called back in 10 minutes with this ratio:

1 day = 1,000 years
1 hour and 40.8 minutes = 70 years

Did you get that? If you lived 70 years, then according to God's "timetable," you would live just over 1 hour and 40 minutes! What are you going to do with it?

As you reflect on your own life, what has the Holy Spirit spoken to you about? Are you living just to be cool? For sports? To drive a nice car or wear nice clothes? Really, what are you living for? Are your priorities worth a hill of beans in light of eternity? If the Lord is speaking to you about something specific, why not respond with a prayer like this:

Jesus, You can reshape my priorities in any way You want. Help me to stabilize my life so that I can see things as You do. Help me to be awakened to what life is really all about and what is really important. I love You, Lord. Teach me how to live! Amen.

Putting it into my life

1. Why is clover compared to having good times exclusive of anything else?
2. Go to your pastor and ask what you can do to help him. Be careful, you may blow his socks right off!
3. Ask your parents how you can be of help to them.
4. Plan to do something that requires solid discipline this week.

WEED 6
Drugs and Alcohol

"Do not gaze at wine when it is red,
when it sparkles in the cup,
when it goes down smoothly!
In the end it bites like a snake
and poisons like a viper" (Proverbs 23:31–32).

Poison ivy appears to be harmless. It is an attractive green plant that can be found in many places. At first glance, it can be mistaken for the popular house plant called the Wandering Jew. But should a person handle it or even just brush up against it, the result can be painful itching and swelling. Once a person is infected, the rash can spread all over his or her body — even to other people. It can cause deep infection and leave scars, and if it gets into the bloodstream, it can cause serious problems.

Alcohol and drugs are like that. They often appear to be harmless — something anyone would want to have around the house. Yet no matter how attractive they might appear, alcohol and drugs are deadly — physically and spiritually.

Scripture warns us about alcohol:

Who has woe? Who has sorrow?

Who has strife? Who has complaints?
Who has needless bruises? Who has bloodshot
eyes?
Those who linger over wine,
who go to sample bowls of mixed wine. (Proverbs
23:29–30)

Indeed, wine betrays him;
he is arrogant and never at rest. (Habakkuk 2:5a)

People who first try drugs or alcohol, no doubt, think
they can control their actions. But we know the opposite
to be true. Think for a minute of the following alcohol-
related statistics reported in a November 30, 1987 issue of
TIME:

- Alcoholism is the third largest health problem in
America today. Every year 26,000 people die from it.
- There are 18 million Americans with a drinking problem.
- Alcohol costs $117 billion a year in everything from
medical expenses to lost workdays.
- Cirrhosis of the liver killed 14,000 people in 1986 – a
direct result of alcohol.
- Drunken drivers were responsible for half of the 46,000
driving fatalities in the U.S. in 1986.
- Alcohol was a factor in up to 70 percent of the 4,000
drowning deaths and in about 30 percent of the nearly
30,000 suicides in 1986.
- It is estimated that one-third of the nation's 523,000
state prison inmates drank heavily before committing
rapes, burglaries and assaults.

Look, too, at these drug-related statistics.

- Marijuana—a drug many feel is relatively harmless—affects a wide range of coordination and mental skills, greatly impairing the ability to drive and run machinery safely. It can also trigger what is referred to as "acute panic/anxiety reaction"—an extreme fear of losing control.
- The long-term side affects of using amphetamines are malnutrition, skin disorders, ulcers, sleeplessness, weight loss, depression and even brain damage.
- Cocaine use affects people in different ways but here are some of the dangers: feelings of restlessness, irritability, anxiety, sleeplessness, paranoia. Moreover, cocaine is highly addictive and demanding; it has caused users to abandon friends, family, hopes and dreams.[4]

When you consider these things, it is a wonder that anyone would allow alcohol or drugs to be part of his or her life, especially a Christian!

The problem is still there, however. Why? Because in every case I have dealt with or heard about, one or all of the following reasons were involved:

Problems. People drink or use drugs because they want to escape problems. Figures indicate that as much as 25 percent of America's teens and young adults use alcohol or drugs to help them handle difficult problems. Even funeral homes are beginning to set up bars to help the bereaved cope with their grief. The fallacy of this is that the drinks or the drugs soon wear off, but the problems are still there.

Feelings of power. People drink or use drugs to feel important. It tells others that "I can handle this." As a kid, I remember watching old westerns on television. I was impressed with the cowboys who would swallow a drink in one big gulp and then slam the glass down on the bar, ordering the bartender to pour them another. What tremendous power they seemed to convey. Today's "cowboys" are the professional athletes who appear on beer advertisements. They lend credence to the notion that drinking beer makes you important.

But what are they really saying? The truth is that more and more professional atheletes are in trouble over alcohol and drugs. It seems that every week we hear of another figure who has been suspended or, worse yet, who has died. How powerful are they when this happens?

Peer pressure. A third reason people let drugs or alcohol become part of their lives is because they get caught in the crunch of peer pressure.

One of our youth group members, Mary, found herself being influenced by peer pressure. She started by drinking a few beers on Friday nights with "friends." Soon she found herself drinking before or after tense situations. Within a few short years, she was unable to relax naturally, and by the age of 17, she was an alcoholic.

What can be done? If you are going to pull up the weed of drugs and alcohol, you must have a plan. No war—and that's what winning over drugs and alcohol is, a war—is ever won without a plan of battle. Consider the following:

1. *Decide to say no before the situation arises*. When mapping out a trip, you often decide to take a specific route. You know which roads will take you to your desti-

nation and which ones won't. The reason you plan ahead is so you can avoid the wrong roads.

Similarly, in "mapping out" your life, you want to avoid the wrong roads. You can see the ruined lives, the shattered homes and the heartache of the many who didn't heed the warning signs of alcohol and drugs. The plan is to avoid at all costs the chance of allowing alcohol and drugs to wreck your life.

Decisions like this demand maturity. They are difficult to make when you are staring temptation eyeball to eyeball. That is why a predetermined *no* is so important. I agree with what Benjamin Franklin said: "It is easier to suppress the first desire than to satisfy all that follow it."

2. *Be friendly but firm in your negative reply to friends' offer of a "drink" or a "smoke."* Drugs and alcohol, especially, are such a part of people's lives in our society that it would be almost unthinkable for a host not to offer his or her guests something to drink or "something to help them relax." Teens have picked up on the same thinking – they offer their friends a beer or a whiff off of a marijuana cigarette or a snort of cocaine. They are just trying to be friendly. How should you reply to their offer?

When I was in college, I worked in construction. I was often asked if I wanted a beer. Always, my answer was no. And you know what, those rough workmen respected my decision. In fact, because I said no, I had a great opportunity to share with many of the 120 men on our crew what Jesus meant in my life. On my last day on the job before I had to leave to return to college, about 40 of the men lined up to shake my hand. They thanked me for being strong enough to say no to alcohol, yet open enough to relate to them. Throughout that summer, I had prayed with several of them about their troubled marriages or their sick children. I had that rapport because I was friendly though firm in maintaining my standards. I believe that is how Jesus reacted. Sinners were not fearful of coming to Him, because they were aware of His great compassion for them.

3. *Decide now what kind of people you are going to spend time with.* Remember the old saying, "Birds of a feather flock together"? Well, it's still true. Paul nailed it down in First Corinthians 15:33: "Do not be misled: 'Bad company corrupts good character.'" If you spend leisure time with others who drink and use drugs, you are asking for trouble. Get out of those relationships—fast!

4. *Be prepared for rejection.* Nobody likes to be rejected. It is one of the greatest fears people have, especially teenagers. But we often have to face it. What one person in the New Testament faced rejection more than Paul. But look how God cared for him and used him mightily—God never let Paul down.

Standing strong for the Lord against drugs and alcohol is not always easy—especially in a day when both are so prevalent in our society. But just as you would avoid poison ivy, so should you avoid drugs and alcohol. If you are going to be 100 percent for God, drugs and alcohol cannot be part of your life. He gives courage to those who would agree with Him on this, and blesses those who say,

> Lord, You're right. I am making my life free of dope and drink. Make my life count for You as I take this stand. I need Your courage; I accept Your call. Thank You, Lord.

Will you take that stand today?

Drugs and Alcohol

Putting it into my life

1. Look again at the statistics on the damage drugs and alcohol are causing in America. Think about examples from your own life or from the lives of people you know.
2. Pledge anew to stay away from drugs and alcohol.
3. Call someone on the phone and share your goal with him or her.

WEED 7

Low Self-Esteem

"He brought me out into a spacious place;
he rescued me because he delighted in me"
(2 Samuel 22:20).

Milkweed is attractive. It grows almost anywhere and is often mistaken for a wild flower. Milkweed is a terror to dairy farmers, though. If cows eat too much of this weed, it will cause their milk to taste bitter and go sour faster. So farmers attack milkweed like Pete Rose attacks baseball—with all their might! If it is allowed to sprout, it causes big problems and costs big bucks.

When I first heard about milkweed and the way it affects cows, I thought, "How could that be? How could a bunch of chewed-up, flowerlike twigs affect the entire milk production of a 1,300 pound cow?" I was skeptical. But I found it to be exactly true: milkweed makes milk cows worthless.

Poor self-esteem can be compared to milkweed, and I am confident that just as the weed ruins cows' milk, so too can poor self-esteem ruin teenagers' lives. Too much of this weed can spoil the way teens view themselves, causing their lives to become bitter and sour.

A farmer destroys milkweed with weed-killer, but

how can teens attack low self-esteem? Is there a surefire plan that guarantees the uprooting of this weed from a life? Can a teen ever be relieved from the problems of a poor self-image?

Yes, because God has the answer. Let's look at some reasons for the problem and how it affects people, and then we'll look at Scripture to see what God has to say about low self-esteem.

Low self-esteem—a tough part of life

Josh McDowell says, "If you can think of anyone you would rather be than yourself, you probably have a self-image problem."[5] Have you ever felt that way? What causes people, particularly teens, to want to be someone else? Why do people get so down on themselves?

There are many reasons. Discovering a rip in your pants when you were standing in front of class while giving a speech will do it every time. Picking up a fumbled football and scoring for the other team will do it. Forgetting to pack underwear when you go to camp for two weeks will do it. So will divorce in your family . . . or being told you are ugly (500,000 Americans a year have cosmetic surgery because they want to be more attractive) . . . or being overweight (every year 40 million Americans go on diets) . . . or always being picked last for a team at school . . . or reading the new cheerleader list and not finding your name included . . . or having your "friend" forget your name when you are being introduced . . . or having been molested . . . or being accused of something you didn't do . . . or being caught doing something wrong. It is hard to get over these embarrassing and hurtful times.

Situations like these destroy our self-esteem and make us wish that we were someone else.

That's how Carol felt. She thought she was the only Christian at her school who took a solid stand for Christ, and she was beginning to wonder if God even cared. It was awkward knowing she had no real friends. She didn't want to get in with the wrong crowd, but she was getting desperate. When she came to talk to me, her self-esteem was about a -10, and she doubted if anything was ever going to turn out right for her.

Tim also felt like a zero. All of his life he had been told by his parents that he was a mistake, that he was just another mouth to feed on an already too-tight budget. As we talked, I could see that Tim ached from lack of love. He told me that he had never been hugged by his dad and that his mom constantly complained of being tired of working as a waitress and receiving only lousy tips from cheap customers. Tim wondered why he had ever been born.

As I talk with teens like Tim and Carol, I try to show them how God sees them. What a change comes over them when they see themselves as God does! Carol has found God's Word is encouraging her when she feels all alone. Tim's attitude is improving as he applys God's truth to his bad situation.

Here's what I showed Carol and Tim about low self-esteem and what God thinks about people as individuals. If you struggle with this weed, get ready for some answers that will uproot the problem. I've seen it happen many times in the lives of teenagers, and it will work for you as you dare to look to God for help.

God understands your feelings of inadequacy

God understands how a poor self-image affects people. He knows we have all made mistakes. Yet He still says, "I am with you. Don't be afraid."

Moses and Jeremiah are two key leaders in the Old Testament. They were both told directly by God to do some incredible things. Remarkably, however, both felt inadequate and told God so. Notice how the Lord allows both men to express the low self-esteem they felt.

> The Lord said, "I have indeed seen the misery of my people in Egypt. I have heard them crying out because of their slave drivers, and I am concerned about their suffering. . . . So now, go. I am sending you to Pharaoh to bring my people the Israelites out of Egypt."

Now notice Moses' response.

> But Moses said to God, "Who am I, that I should go to Pharaoh and bring the Israelites out of Egypt?" (Exodus 3:7, 10–11)

Jeremiah felt the same way.

> The word of the Lord came to me, saying
>   "Before I formed you in the womb I knew you,
>   before you were born I set you apart;
>   I appointed you as a prophet to the nations."
>
> "Ah, Sovereign Lord," I said, "I do not know how to speak; I am only a child." (Jeremiah 1:4–6)

There you have it. These two men were afraid they would fail. They did not have the confidence even though God Himself had spoken with them.

Maybe you feel that way also. Whatever the reasons for your feelings of inadequacy, you are wondering whether God cares about you and your insecurity. He does care. I love the way He handles the negative feedback He received from Moses and Jeremiah.

And God said, "I will be with you." (Exodus 3:12)

But the Lord said to me, "Do not say, 'I am only a child.' You must go to everyone I send you to and say whatever I command you. Do not be afraid of them, for I am with you and will rescue you," declares the Lord." (Jeremiah 1:7–8)

What a thrill to know that at the times when we feel the weakest, we can be confident that God Himself is with us! That is not a cheap emotional "high" – it is solid truth.

We are the object of God's attention

In Matthew 6, Jesus is talking to a group of people about how His Father feels about them as individuals. In this first sermon of the New Testament, Christ develops the theme for the rest of God's Word, which is God's love for people. Notice what Jesus says:

Look at the birds of the air, they do not sow or reap or store away in barns, and yet your heavenly Father feeds them. Are you not much more valuable than they? (Matthew 6:26)

What a terrific thought! If God is concerned about the birds of the air, surely He cares for us. What a great way to see yourself—God caring for *you*. That uproots negative self-image and puts it on the trash heap. Why? Because we are the object of God's attention. After all, He did send His only Son to earth to die for our sin, didn't He?

That kind of love was hard for me to grasp, but one Easter Sunday morning I began to understand it. My wife Kay awakened me at 4:16 and said, "It's time to go." I couldn't imagine what she was talking about, but then I remembered that she was pregnant. "It's time to go" probably meant that it was time to go to the hospital!

Sure enough, she was in labor. After we arrived at the hospital, she was taken to the maternity floor and a few hours later delivered our first baby—a boy. I was the first to hold Les, Jr., after he had been checked over. His little fingers wrapped around mine, and he stopped crying as soon as I talked to him. I remember feeling the sense of wonder at having a son and being a Dad for the first time. Later that evening, Kay and I prayed together. We were so excited about our little boy! As we held hands in her room, thanking the Lord for this new little life, it hit me like a two by four between the eyes. God had sent His *little boy* for me. That first Easter was the ultimate demonstration of God's love for me—Jesus rising from the dead, canceling sin and offering forgiveness, all for me! All I could do was weep with joy. I was the object of God's attention!

God doesn't compare us with anyone else

We have said two things about low self-esteem. First, God is with us no matter what and He understands our weaknesses. Second, we are the object of His attention. Next, we need to understand that the Lord doesn't compare us with anyone else. We are so unique, that He threw away the mold after He made us. There is no one like you. You are *you*.

When I first heard this, I wanted proof. Philippians 1:6 had the answer: "Being confident of this, that he who began a good work in you will carry it on to completion until the day of Christ Jesus." What a discovery! God is working on me as though I am His personal project.

What a relief to know this! For years I felt that I was the oddball of the family. My two brothers and sister all have fantastic skills in art. They have all received awards for their efforts. Naturally people thought I would have these same gifts. What a joke! My handwriting is so bad that my secretary had to study Egyptian to understand what I scratch out on paper. But guess what? God doesn't compare me with my brothers or sister or anyone else. He is working on *me*, not so I can match skills or looks or brains or anything else with others, but so that I can be the best *me*. No comparison!

My friend, Fred Hartley, writes about this same concept. Listen to this:

The first thing we need to understand about ourselves is that we are unique. You can look and look and look and never find another one like you. You are it.

In a sense, we could all wear buttons that say, "Special," "Custom-made," "Handcrafted," "One of a Kind," "An Original," "Made by the Master Craftsman." When God made us, He didn't look through back issues of *Sports Illustrated* or *Seventeen* to come up with ideas. When He creates a woman, He does not take the eyebrows of Brooke Shields, the body of Cheryl Tiegs, the brains of Sandra Day O'Connor and the pedigree of Lady Di. He starts from scratch. When He makes a man, He doesn't take the speed of Carl Lewis, the agility of Doctor J, the stamina of Pete Rose and the tongue of Howard Cosell. After He made them, He threw away their blueprints. And before He made us, He drew up another whole set. We are unique.[6]

It's true, God doesn't compare you with anybody, because no one can be compared to you.

Are you starting to get the picture? God cares for you and understands your feelings of low self-esteem. You are the object of His attention, and He says that you are so special that there is no one like you in the entire world. Incredible, isn't it? The same God who made the earth with all of its different kinds and species decided there would only be one of you. Wow!

We are the apple of God's eye

You know what else I tell teens struggling with a poor self-image? You are the apple of God's eye. When I first heard this, I doubted it. But when I searched the Scriptures, here's what I found: "For this is what the Lord Almighty says: 'After he has honored me and has sent me against the nations that have plundered you—for whoever touches you touches the apple of his eye—I will surely raise up my hand against them so that their slaves will plunder them.'" (Zechariah 2:8).

We are special to God. When God talks like this about His people, He isn't kidding. His love reaches to us at the cost of His Son's life, and He is offended when we are offended.

When I was in the seventh grade, two older teenage boys stopped me on my way home from school one day. They asked me if I had any cigarettes or money. I told them no. Then one turned to the other and asked if he thought I should be beaten up. Fortunately for me, the second kid said no, and I went on my way. When my dad came home for his supper break, I told him what had happened. He looked at me and said, "If you ever see those guys when I am with you, just let me know." With that, the subject was dropped.

On weekends I worked the concession stand at a theater where my dad was the manager. The next Friday night, guess who came in and talked to my dad about a job? You got it—the same two barracudas who had stopped me on the way home from school several days before. Finally I got my dad's attention and let him know that these were the creeps I had told him about. What happened next was as cool as Christmas.

After my dad was sure he knew which boys I was talking about, he told me to pour them a Pepsi and give them anything they wanted free of charge. He then turned to me and said, "Which one was it, son?" I pointed to the kid, and my ex-marine father went bananas.

He reached out and jerked that kid so hard the buttons on his shirt went zipping across the room. With one hand, my dad lifted that kid literally off the ground and brought him up to where he was staring him in the face. With the other hand, he pointed to me and shouted in his drill sergeant voice to this high schooler: "That is my son! If you ever talk to him again the way you did, I will personally come and find you. Now get out of here and don't ever come in my theater again." With that, he shook this punk a few more times, asking him if he understood. When he left, his shirt looked as if it had been pressed in the blender. The last time I saw him, he was hightailing it down the road, looking for a place to hide.

The point I want to make is that when I was offended, my dad was offended too. That night I learned a lesson about my father's feelings toward his children. Someone had touched one of the apples of my dad's eye, and that was a stupid thing to do!

The best part is this: according to Zechariah 2:8, our Heavenly Father is offended when we are and says that whoever offends us, the apples of His eye, will have a direct confrontation with Him! When you begin to see that you are the object of God's attention, that you are unique, that no one compares with you and that you are the apple of His eye, you can't help but see yourself in a new light!

God delights in you

Here's the proof: "He brought me out into a spacious place; he rescued me because he delighted in me" (2 Samuel 22:20). Did you get that? God delights in you! Why? Because there is no one else who can compare with you. You are unique and the object of God's attention. He is delighted to have you as one of His children.

As I was sharing this with my friend Dan, he struggled to believe it. Obviously, his self-esteem was zilch. Crying with deep sobs he said, "Les, if you only knew my past, you wouldn't have the guts to tell me that. There is no way God could ever delight in me. Not now—not in a thousand years!"

As we talked, Dan gradually opened up. He told how he had been drunk so often that he couldn't count the times. He had cheated his way through school, and worst of all, he felt the only way he could be accepted was to be what other people wanted him to be. His need to be liked and wanted led him to believe a homosexual relationship was OK. When his family found out, there was a major confrontation and feelings of bitterness toward him. How could God ever be delighted with him?

I do not comprehend the grace of God or why He desires to reach out to individuals as sinful as we are, but one thing I do know, God delights in people. He longed so deeply to have a relationship with us that He sent His Son Jesus to be our "bridge" back to Him.

It was David who said, "He brought me out into a spacious place; he rescued me because he delighted in me." If ever there was a man who needed God's grace, it was David. He had committed adultery and, to cover his guilt, arranged to have a man killed in battle. He had willfully done wrong. But he repented and God received him back. It was God who rescued him and then delighted in him. David came to God with his sin problem and was forgiven. God delights in our honesty, too, and longs to have us close to Him. I don't know about you, but I want a relationship with a God who loves me *that* much.

In this chapter we have explored briefly some of the reasons why people have low self-esteem. We have also seen that God (1) understands our inadequate feelings; (2) views us as the object of His attention; (3) does not compare us with anyone else; (4) sees us as the apple of His eye; and (5) delights in us. Let me ask you: Will you begin to believe these truths from God's Word? Will you allow the Holy Spirit to root out those milkweeds of poor self-image? Why not begin to make a new life for yourself by looking in the mirror and saying, "God loves me. He is working in me, and I am the apple of His eye." You may not have all the answers, but you do have the promise that God thinks you are sensational!

Putting it into my life

1. Why is milkweed compared to low self-esteem?
2. Review from Scripture the five truths that speak against a poor self-image.
3. Go to the mirror and take a good long look at what God says is an ultimate creation. You aren't junk!
4. Pin the five biblical truths on your bulletin board so that you can review them often.

Scripture— God's Weedkiller

"Blessed is the man
who does not walk in the counsel
of the wicked
or stand in the way of sinners
or sit in the seat of mockers.
But his delight is in the law of the Lord,
and on his law he meditates day and night.
He is like a tree planted by streams of water,
which yields its fruit in season
and whose leaf does not wither.
Whatever he does prospers" (Psalm 1:1–3).

We have talked about a number of "weeds" that can smother a teen's effort to walk with Jesus Christ. I mentioned in the opening chapter that being a strong Christian is not easy. It is tough to be different. But those who do go this route have a confidence in their stride that clearly says, "I'm going God's way, and I am going to win!" In John 8:31–32, Jesus told His hearers what the result of following Him would be: "If you hold to my teaching, you are really my disciples. Then you will know the truth, and the truth will set you free."

Throughout this book, I have related many stories of teens who have been trapped in rebellion and peer pressure, of teens who succumbed to an unchecked thought life, of individuals tricked by the appeal of drugs and alcohol. Yet God is still calling young people into a lifestyle that resists the attitude that says, "Where's the next party?"

So, how do we keep advancing? That is the question that many teens want answered. To advance spiritually, we must make Scripture a vital part of our lives. Without God's "weed-killer," we cannot rid ourselves of the harmful weeds that try to crop up in our lives and keep us from achieving our best for God. Let's look at why Scripture is so important in our walk with Christ and then set up a strategy on how to implement it in our lives.

Scripture–the tool for winners over weeds

Scripture is the hoe that removes the weeds from our lives and allows us to keep growing in God's ways. David said in Psalm 119:11, "I have hidden your word in my heart that I might not sin against you." In that sentence alone we see several important concepts.

Notice how it begins: "*I* [italics mine] have hidden." No one could read the Scripture for David. That was his job. The same is true for us today. As growing Christians, we have to make time for the Bible to be a part of our lives. No one else can do it for us.

I remember the day I met my wife, Kay. It was my first day and first class of college. She walked into the classroom, and I about fell out of my chair. She was one of the most beautiful girls I had ever seen. I remember thinking, "I need to get to know that girl–*right* away!" My excitement quickly faded, however, with what I saw next—she was holding hands with another guy! I was devastated! Here was this gorgeous girl—the girl of my dreams—attached to this other man. He was a little short fellow—just 5' 19" tall—the starting center for the college basketball team. What was I to do except to wait it out and hope for the best.

After a while—three years!—she saw the error of her ways, and we had our first date. During those three years, I discovered that Kay was more than just beautiful on the outside—she had inner beauty, too! She loved the Lord fervently, and her Bible proved it. It was torn, marked up, cried over, dog-eared and had only half of its cover. The first time I saw it, I wondered if she had been playing punt, pass and kick with it. I soon discovered the reason for her inner beauty—she spent time with her Bible, and she was faithful in asking the Lord to make her the woman He wanted her to be. After being married to her for nearly nine years, I still think she is a "knockout." But her finest quality is her love for the Lord and for His Word. She is truly a woman of God.

For any teenager who wants to be God's man or woman, spending time in prayer and Bible-reading is a must. No one can do it for you. Your youth pastor can't do it for you; neither can your Sunday school teacher, basketball coach, band leader, parents, girlfriend or boyfriend—no one.

Look at what David did—he hid the Word of God in his heart. When the Bible speaks of the heart, it is talking about the core of a person—the inner man or woman. There are many things that can be hidden in our hearts: dirty jokes, immoral thoughts, bitterness toward our parents. In Psalm 119:11, David pledged to hide God's Word in his heart so that the "real" David would live a life that was pleasing to God, even when no one was looking. That is what God is looking for today.

Blake is determined to be just that kind of teen. He is a senior in high school who is blessed with unusual sports abilities. His upper body strength is awesome, and when he walks into a room, the girls take notice. But the best part of Blake is his dogged determination to live life as the Bible defines it.

Blake's parents are missionaries to jungle people in Irian Jaya, Indonesia. As a youth, he witnessed whole tribes of people coming to Christ. During sociology class one day, Blake was asked to share some of his jungle growing-up experiences. Even though this was a public school, Blake didn't back down. He told how the people were changed from a Stone-age, animistic and, in some cases, cannibalistic people, and he attributed the change to God and His mighty power. After he finished talking, he was asked if the Bible made any difference in his life. Without hesitation, he told the class how he gets up early every morning to read his Bible and pray. The result is that he dates differently, thinks differently, lives differently – he views life from God's perspective.

No question about it. Blake is on fire for God because he spends time in the Scriptures. He has one goal – to be God's man. Nothing ignites him like that challenge. That thought is like dynamite to him. It blasts him out of bed every morning and gets him moving. Blake is alive for God because he reads the Word of God and because he hides it in his heart!

Look back at our Scripture verse. Why did David hide

God's Word in his heart? So that he wouldn't sin against God. Isn't that incredible! If we take the time to make God's Word our standard, we will have a relationship with God that will keep us from wanting to sin against Him.

I married Kay on May 19, 1979. That day, I pledged to her my dedication, my love and my intent to always remain true to her. To this day, I have not intentionally violated that trust. During our years together, I have discovered what offends her and what she likes. When I do offend her, I can usually detect it immediately, and I go to her, apologize, and we get on with living again in harmony.

The same is true in our relationship with God. As we read His Word, we learn to understand His ways. When we offend Him, we can recognize it, apologize for it and resume our relationship.

We have seen why it is so important to use the tool of Scripture in our lives. It keeps us sharp and aware of God's will, and it allows us to live in harmony with God. Now let's set up a strategy on how to put Scripture into our daily living.

God's Word in my life

Teens are in one of four categories when it comes to Scripture reading. They either (a) read the Bible on a regular basis, (b) try to read it on a regular basis, (c) want to read it on a regular basis or (d) don't read it at all. The counterpart to all this is: (a) you can improve, (b) you can succeed, (c) you can be shown how to do it or (d) you need to be challenged to be different.

Today many teens—and adults—are struggling when it comes to reading the Bible on a regular basis. Many people, in fact, are totally ignorant when it comes to Bible knowledge. On a recent quiz, 7 out of 10 could not answer the following questions:

1. Name the four gospels.
2. How many disciples were there?
3. What is the reason we celebrate Easter?

The sad fact about those who took this simple quiz was that 43 percent of the Christian kids could not answer the questions correctly. Nineteen percent didn't know *any* of the answers!

Should this lack of knowledge characterize a Christian? Absolutely not! Here's what God says about those who know His Word:

Blessed is the man
　who does not walk in the counsel of the wicked
or stand in the way of sinners
　or sit in the seat of mockers.
But his delight is in the law of the Lord,
　and on his law he meditates day and night. (Psalm
　1:1–2)

What a difference it makes to have Scripture in your life! It is to be to us a joy and a delight to read the Word of God. Jeremiah spoke of it as being as delightful as eating.

When your words came, I ate them;
　they were my joy and my heart's delight,
for I bear your name,
　O Lord God Almighty. (Jeremiah 15:16)

Anytime teenagers do not eat at least every 20 minutes or so, something is wrong. Only a few things can make them lose their appetites:

• they just got jilted by a boy or girlfriend
• the team listing did not include their name
• they got caught flushing cherry bombs down a school toilet
• the Clearasil isn't working
• the Algebra test looked like something from another planet
• family troubles are brewing

Reading the Bible should be as natural to us as eating. It should be both a necessity and a source of joy. When we don't spend time reading God's Word, we aren't prepared for spiritual battle, and we will not be dynamic Christians.

A letter from the President

While I was serving as youth pastor in Port Charlotte, Florida, Ronald Reagan was reelected as President of the United States. There were about 40 kids in our youth group who wrote to congratulate him and to tell him that we would be praying for him. As I was bundling up those letters for mailing, I remember thinking, *Wouldn't it be cool if the president wrote to us. Really, Lord, how many youth groups get a letter from the President of the United States? Those kids would flip.*

When I opened the mailbox 10 days later, I nearly fainted. In it was a letter from the President. I read it at the next youth group meeting, amid the cheering and clapping of an exuberant bunch of kids. A letter from the President of the United States was too much!

Guess what I talked on that night after the celebration was over. You got it—the Bible and its importance in our lives. I pointed out that just as it was an incredible experience to receive a letter from the White House, so it ought to be with the Bible. We have a chance every day to read a letter sent to us by Almighty God!

Too long?

"I would like to read the Bible, but it's just too long. I can't really get excited about it." I often hear teens say this. Jack Hayford, a radio pastor in California, once said that we shouldn't think of the Bible as a *big* book. He gave some interesting "Bible-size" statistics. If you read Isaiah, Job, Psalms, Ezekiel, Genesis and Exodus, you have read nearly 40 percent of Bible. There are five books of the Bible with only one chapter. (Want to impress your youth pastor? Call him up and say that you have just finished reading five books of the Bible. Don't tell him that the books you read had only one chapter each. One word of caution is due: better plan to have the nitro tablets near. Your message may just send him on.) Of the 66 books, 38 can be read in less than an hour, and 24 have fewer than 5 chapters. Does that make the Bible seem smaller?

Devise a system

Systematically reading through the Bible during a year is one good way to make Scripture reading a regular part of your life. I often hear teens say that their New Year's resolution is to read through the Bible during the coming year. To do this, they plan to read about three chapters a day. By about January 20, however, they are usually 25 chapters behind schedule. Result? Frustration and guilt. "How could I have let God down so badly? He is probably thinking, 'What a jerk'."

Tom felt that way. It was a relief to him when he discovered that while God does say we should read day and night, He never states that a specific amount of time or a certain number of pages are required. That would be bondage, and it would leave people feeling that performance is what God is looking for. The opposite is true. God is looking for those who *want* to read the Bible—not those who do it because they feel they *have* to. There is a big difference in the two approaches.

Look at these facts about Bible reading:

- If you read three chapters a day, you will need to read for 376 days—10 days longer than any leap year. I don't think God will blow a fuse over your taking that schedule, though.
- If you read five chapters a day, you can read the Bible through in eight months.
- If you read for one hour a day, you can read the Bible through in less than three months.
- If you take less than 12 minutes a day, you can read it through in a year.

The key to Scripture reading is to set your own pace.

"But Les, what about all those genealogies and long lists? How do I get through those?" Let's be honest. Some of those parts are boring, but the encouraging thing is that of the 1,189 chapters in the Bible, only about 80 are like this. That is less than 6.7 percent. When you look at it like that, it is much easier to work your way through them.

Scripture – God's "Weedkiller"

We have seen how important Scripture reading is to those who want to pursue God. We have also considered some specific facts about making Scripture reading a part of our lives. I want to leave with you the story of one teenager who was being smothered by the weeds in his life and how he found relief in God's Word.

This teenager's family was successful and involved at a high level in the political scene. He was attending a prestigious school and was popular. With his privileges, family heritage and natural charisma, he had it made—or so it seemed on the outside. But on the inside, this young man was completely empty. Despair became his constant state of mind.

One day he became so sick of his life that he decided to end it. He swallowed poisonous chemicals and lost consciousness. When he came to, he found himself in a hospital room, surrounded by his concerned family.

During his stay in the hospital, he had time to reflect on his life. He knew his parents were concerned for him, but they didn't really understand his despair. Then someone brought him a Bible.

Because his body was dehydrated, he couldn't sit up. So he asked his mother to read to him. As she read, something happened inside him; never had he felt such comfort and hope. He became intrigued with this person, Jesus Christ. Then he heard these words from John 14: "Because I live, you also will live" (verse 19b). That was it! He knew the resurrected Jesus alone could help, and he prayed to receive Him as his Savior.

From that moment, things in his life began to change. He now had a reason to live—and a message to tell to the world. He started sharing Jesus with friends and relatives as God gave him opportunities. Soon, he was being asked to speak at youth groups and in evangelistic meetings. By the time he was 19, he won the Asian Youth Preacher Award. He was on the move for God!

He has continued to maintain a strong walk with Christ for more than 20 years, speaking frequently at universities and colleges literally around the world. In 1983, Billy Graham sponsored a meeting in Amsterdam for evangelists from all over the world. More than 4,000 attended that conference, and every continent on earth was represented. This man, who at age 17 had attempted to take his life, was invited to be one of the key speakers at this conference. When the conference was held again in 1986, more than 10,000 people attended! It was the largest gathering of internationals in the world. This same man was once again asked to speak. He has had an incredible ministry!

What made the change in this once hopeless teenager? What makes someone rise up from a bed of suicide to go literally around the world to speak of Jesus Christ? For Ravi Zacharias, the difference was that the Word of God had redefined his reason for living. He pulled the weed of despair, and allowed the Scriptures to propel him forward with a life-changing message that offered hope to those who would respond as he had.

The bottom line to all this is — what really causes you to live the way you do? Is it to make a name in sports? Is it to impress a girl or boyfriend? Is it to be accepted by the group of people whom you admire? There is only one *real* reason to live, however. It is Jesus. As we pledge our lives to Him, He calls us to take the Word of God as our standard and to let it be the thing by which we live.

Will you let that be the goal of your life? Begin today to pull all the weeds and uproot the useless things that are robbing you of being your best for God. It begins by allowing Scripture to be your guide in life and by saying yes to the Holy Spirit. He will guide you and show you what must be uprooted so you can grow to the maximum for God. Determination to be God's man or woman demands listening and obeying. Will you take the challenge and be that person?

NOTES

1. Charles R. Swindoll, *Strengthening Your Grip* (Waco, Texas: Word Books, 1982), p. 237.

2. Fred Hartley, *Dare to Be Different* (Old Tappan, New Jersey: Fleming H. Revell Company, 1980), pp. 14–15.

3. Dr. Gary R. Collins, "Teenage Problems," Christian Counselor's Library, Editor Tape 13.

4. Chris Lutes, *What Teenagers Are Saying about Drugs & Alcohol* (Wheaton: Campus Life Books, 1987), pp. 27–33.

5. Josh McDowell, *His Image . . . My Image* (San Bernardino, California: Here's Life Publishers, Inc., 1984), p. 11.

6. Fred Hartley, *Flops* (New Jersey, Old Tappan: Fleming H. Revell Company, 1985), pp. 63–64.